GREAT KEYBOARD SONATAS

Carl Philipp Emanuel BACH

Series I

Dover Publications, Inc.
NEW YORK

CONTENTS

The present volume contains sonatas composed between 1731 and 1751. The sequence is by year of composition. Only those years of first publication are given that fall within the composer's lifetime or the first generation after his death. The W numbers are those assigned to the sonatas in the standard work by Alfred Wotquenne, *Thematisches Verzeichnis der Werke von Carl Philipp Emanuel Bach (1714–1788)*, Leipzig, 1905.

Sonata in B-flat Major, W.62/1 (composed Leipzig 1731, revised Berlin 1744, published Berlin 1761 in *Musikalisches Allerley*)	1
Sonata in G Major, W.65/6 (composed Frankfurt 1736, revised Berlin 1743)	7
Sonata in G Minor, W.65/11 (composed Berlin 1739, published Berlin 1792 in *Trois Sonates*)	13
"Prussian" Sonatas, W.48/1–6 (composed Berlin 1740–1742, published Nuremberg 1742 or 1743 as *Sei Sonate per Cembalo, che all'Augusta Maestà di Federico II, Re di Prussia . . .*)	20
F Major, W.48/1	20
B-flat Major, W.48/2	24
E Major, W.48/3	32
C Minor, W.48/4	38
C Major, W.48/5	44
A Major, W.48/6	50
Sonata in B Minor, W.65/13 (composed Töplitz 1743)	60
Sonata in E Major, W.62/5 (composed Berlin 1744, published Nuremberg 1760–1763 in *Œuvres mêlées*)	68
Sonata in D Minor, W.62/4 (composed Berlin 1744, published Nuremberg 1760–1763 in *Œuvres mêlées*)	77
Sonata in F Minor, W.62/6 (composed Berlin 1744, published Berlin 1761 in *Musikalisches Allerley*)	84
Sonata in C Major, W.62/7 (composed Berlin 1744, published Nuremberg 1760–1761 in *Collection récréative*)	92
"Württemberg" Sonatas, W.49/1–6 (composed Berlin 1742–1744, published Nuremberg 1744 as *Sei Sonate per Cembalo, dedicate all'Altezza Serenissima di Carlo Eugenio, Duca di Wirtemberg . . .*)	98
A Minor, W.49/1	98
A-flat Major, W.49/2	108
E Minor, W.49/3	116
B-flat Major, W.49/4	122
E-flat Major, W.49/5	129
B Minor, W.49/6	137
Sonata in B-flat Major, W.65/20 (composed Berlin 1747, published Vienna and Leipzig ca. 1802 in *Grande Sonate*)	147
Sonata in F Major, W.62/8 (composed Potsdam 1748, published Berlin 1762 in *Tonstücke für das Clavier*)	159
Sonata in D Minor, W.65/24 (composed Berlin 1749)	166
Sonata in F Major, W.62/9 (composed Berlin 1749, published Nuremberg 1760–1763 in *Œuvres mêlées*)	170
Sonata in C Major, W.62/10 (composed Berlin 1749, published Berlin 1762–1763 in *Musikalisches Mancherley*)	176
Sonata in E Minor, W.62/12 (composed Berlin 1751, published Berlin 1761 in *Musikalisches Allerley*)	182

Copyright © 1985 by Dover Publications, Inc.
All rights reserved under Pan American and International Copyright Conventions.

Published in Canada by General Publishing Company, Ltd., 30 Lesmill Road, Don Mills, Toronto, Ontario.
Published in the United Kingdom by Constable and Company, Ltd., 10 Orange Street, London WC2H 7EG.

This Dover edition, first published in 1985, is a new selection, arranged in a new sequence, of sonatas by C. P. E. Bach as published within Volumes XII and XIII of *Le Trésor des Pianistes*, edited by Aristide and Louise Farrenc, Paris, 1861–1874. Series I of the Dover edition contains sonatas composed between 1731 and 1751; Series II, sonatas composed between 1752 and 1784. See the table of contents for original publication years of the various sonatas, original composition years and Wotquenne numbers.

Manufactured in the United States of America
Dover Publications, Inc., 31 East 2nd Street, Mineola, N.Y. 11501

Library of Congress Cataloging in Publication Data

Bach, Carl Philipp Emanuel, 1714–1788.
 [Sonatas, keyboard instrument. Selections]
 Great keyboard sonatas.

 (v. of music)
 Originally published in v. 12–13 of Le trésor des pianistes, edited by Aristide and Louise Farrenc, Paris, 1861–1874.
 1. Sonatas (Harpsichord) 2. Sonatas (Clavichord) 3. Sonatas (Piano) I. Title.
 M23.B12F4 1985   84-759591
 ISBN 0-486-24853-4 (v. 1)
 ISBN 0-486-24854-2 (v. 2)

Sonata in B-flat Major, W.62/1

Sonata in B-flat Major, W.62/1

Sonata in B-flat Major, W.62/1

Sonata in B-flat Major, W.62/1

Sonata in G Major, W.65/6

8 Sonata in G Major, W.65/6

Sonata in G Major, W.65/6

Sonata in G Major, W.65/6

12 Sonata in G Major, W.65/6

Sonata in G Minor, W.65/11

Sonata in G Minor, W.65/11

Sonata in G Minor, W.65/11

Sonata in G Minor, W. 65/11

Sonata in F Major, W.48/1 ("Prussian" 1)

Sonata in F Major, W. 48/1 ("Prussian" 1)

Sonata in F Major, W.48/1 ("Prussian" 1)

Sonata in B-flat Major, W. 48/2 ("Prussian" 2)

Sonata in B-flat Major, W.48/2 ("Prussian" 2)

Sonata in B-flat Major, W. 48/2 ("Prussian" 2)

28 Sonata in B-flat Major, W. 48/2 ("Prussian" 2)

Sonata in B-flat Major, W. 48/2 ("Prussian" 2)

Sonata in B-flat Major, W. 48/2 ("Prussian" 2)

Sonata in E Major, W.48/3 ("Prussian" 3)

Sonata in E Major, W. 48/3 ("Prussian" 3)

Sonata in E Major, W. 48/3 ("Prussian" 3)

Sonata in E Major, W. 48/3 ("Prussian" 3)

Sonata in E Major, W. 48/3 ("Prussian" 3)

Sonata in C Minor, W.48/4 ("Prussian" 4)

Sonata in C Minor, W. 48/4 ("Prussian" 4)

Sonata in C Minor, W. 48/4 ("Prussian" 4)

Sonata in C Minor, W. 48/4 ("Prussian" 4)

Sonata in C Major, W.48/5 ("Prussian" 5)

Poco Allegro.

Sonata in C Major, W. 48/5 ("Prussian" 5)

Sonata in C Major, W. 48/5 ("Prussian" 5)

48 Sonata in C Major, W. 48/5 ("Prussian" 5)

Sonata in A Major, W.48/6 ("Prussian" 6)

Sonata in A Major, W. 48/6 ("Prussian" 6)

52 Sonata in A Major, W. 48/6 ("Prussian" 6)

Sonata in A Major, W. 48/6 ("Prussian" 6)

Sonata in A Major, W. 48/6 ("Prussian" 6)

58 Sonata in A Major, W.48/6 ("Prussian" 6)

Sonata in A Major, W. 48/6 ("Prussian" 6)

Sonata in B Minor, W.65/13

Sonata in B Minor, W.65/13

Sonata in B Minor, W.65/13

64 Sonata in B Minor, W.65/13

Sonata in B Minor, W.65/13

Sonata in B Minor, W.65/13

Sonata in B Minor, W.65/13

Sonata in E Major, W.62/5

Sonata in E Major, W.62/5

76 Sonata in E Major, W. 62/5

Sonata in D Minor, W.62/4

ANDANTE SOSTENUTO.

Sonata in D Minor, W.62/4

Sonata in D Minor, W.62/4

Sonata in D Minor, W.62/4

Sonata in F Minor, W.62/6

Sonata in F Minor, W.62/6

86 Sonata in F Minor, W.62/6

Sonata in F Minor, W.62/6

Sonata in F Minor, W. 62/6

Sonata in F Minor, W. 62/6

Sonata in C Major, W.62/7

Allegro assai.

Sonata in C Major, W.62/7

Sonata in C Major, W.62/7

Sonata in C Major, W.62/7

Sonata in C Major, W.62/7

Sonata in A Minor, W.49/1 ("Württemberg" 1)

Sonata in A Minor, W. 49/1 ("Württemberg" 1)

Sonata in A Minor, W. 49/1 ("Württemberg" 1)

Sonata in A Minor, W. 49/1 ("Württemberg" 1)

Sonata in A Minor, W. 49/1 ("Württemberg" 1)

Sonata in A Minor, W. 49/1 ("Württemberg" 1)

ALLEGRO ASSAI.

104 Sonata in A Minor, W. 49/1 ("Württemberg" 1)

106 Sonata in A Minor, W.49/1 ("Württemberg" 1)

Sonata in A Minor, W. 49/1 ("Württemberg" 1)

Sonata in A-flat Major, W.49/2 ("Württemberg" 2)

Sonata in A-flat Major, W. 49/2 ("Württemberg" 2)

110 Sonata in A-flat Major, W. 49/2 ("Württemberg" 2)

Sonata in A-flat Major, W. 49/2 ("Württemberg" 2)

112 Sonata in A-flat Major, W. 49/2 ("Württemberg" 2)

Sonata in A-flat Major, W. 49/2 ("Württemberg" 2)

Sonata in A-flat Major, W. 49/2 ("Württemberg" 2)

Sonata in A-flat Major, W. 49/2 ("Württemberg" 2)

Sonata in E Minor, W.49/3 ("Württemberg" 3)

Sonata in E Minor, W. 49/3 ("Württemberg" 3)

118 Sonata in E Minor, W. 49/3 ("Württemberg" 3)

Sonata in E Minor, W. 49/3 ("Württemberg" 3)

Sonata in E Minor, W. 49/3 ("Württemberg" 3)

Sonata in E Minor, W. 49/3 ("Württemberg" 3)

Sonata in B-flat Major, W.49/4 ("Württemberg" 4)

Sonata in B-flat Major, W. 49/4 ("Württemberg" 4)

124 Sonata in B-flat Major, W. 49/4 ("Württemberg" 4)

Sonata in B-flat Major, W. 49/4 ("Württemberg" 4)

126 Sonata in B-flat Major, W. 49/4 ("Württemberg" 4)

128 Sonata in B-flat Major, W.49/4 ("Württemberg" 4)

Sonata in E-flat Major, W.49/5 ("Württemberg" 5)

130 Sonata in E-flat Major, W. 49/5 ("Württemberg" 5)

Sonata in E-flat Major, W. 49/5 ("Württemberg" 5)

Sonata in E-flat Major, W. 49/5 ("Württemberg" 5)

Sonata in E-flat Major, W. 49/5 ("Württemberg" 5)

134 Sonata in E-flat Major, W. 49/5 ("Württemberg" 5)

136　Sonata in E-flat Major, W. 49/5 ("Württemberg" 5)

Sonata in B Minor, W.49/6 ("Württemberg" 6)

Sonata in B Minor, W. 49/6 ("Württemberg" 6)

Sonata in B Minor, W. 49/6 ("Württemberg" 6)

Sonata in B Minor, W. 49/6 ("Württemberg" 6)

Sonata in B Minor, W. 49/6 ("Württemberg" 6)

142 Sonata in B Minor, W. 49/6 ("Württemberg" 6)

Sonata in B Minor, W.49/6 ("Württemberg" 6)

Sonata in B Minor, W. 49/6 ("Württemberg" 6)

Sonata in B Minor, W. 49/6 ("Württemberg" 6)

146　Sonata in B Minor, W. 49/6 ("Württemberg" 6)

Sonata in B-flat Major, W.65/20

Sonata in B-flat Major, W.65/20

Sonata in B-flat Major, W.65/20

Sonata in B-flat Major, W.65/20

Sonata in B-flat Major, W.65/20

152 Sonata in B-flat Major, W.65/20

Sonata in B-flat Major, W.65/20

Sonata in B-flat Major, W.65/20

Sonata in B-flat Major, W.65/20

Sonata in B-flat Major, W.65/20

158 Sonata in B-flat Major, W.65/20

Sonata in F Major, W.62/8

160 Sonata in F Major, W.62/8

Sonata in F Major, W. 62/8

Sonata in D Minor, W.65/24

168 Sonata in D Minor, W.65/24

Sonata in F Major, W.62/9

Sonata in F Major, W. 62/9

Sonata in F Major, W. 62/9

174 Sonata in F Major, W.62/9

Sonata in C Major, W.62/10

Sonata in C Major, W.62/10

Sonata in C Major, W.62/10

Sonata in C Major, W.62/10

Sonata in C Major, W.62/10

Sonata in C Major, W.62/10

Sonata in E Minor, W.62/12

Allemande.

Courante.

Sonata in E Minor, W.62/12

Sarabande.

Sonata in E Minor, W.62/12

Sonata in E Minor, W.62/12

Menuet 3.

Sonata in E Minor, W.62/12

Gigue.

188 Sonata in E Minor, W.62/12

Sonata in E Minor, W.62/12

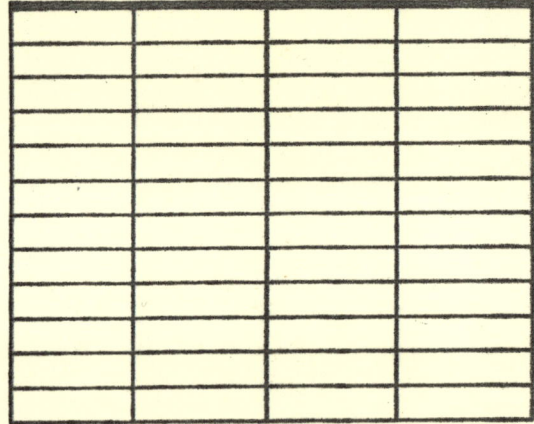